To Wilfrid Wood

First published 2012 by Walker Books Ltd, 87 Vauxhall Walk, London SE11 5HJ

2 4 6 8 10 9 7 5 3 1   © 2012 David Lucas

This book has been typeset in Berkeley Old Style   Printed in China

British Library Cataloguing in Publication Data: a catalogue record for this book is available from the British Library

ISBN 978-1-4063-1505-9   www.walker.co.uk

WALKER BOOKS

AND SUBSIDIARIES

LONDON • BOSTON • SYDNEY • AUCKLAND

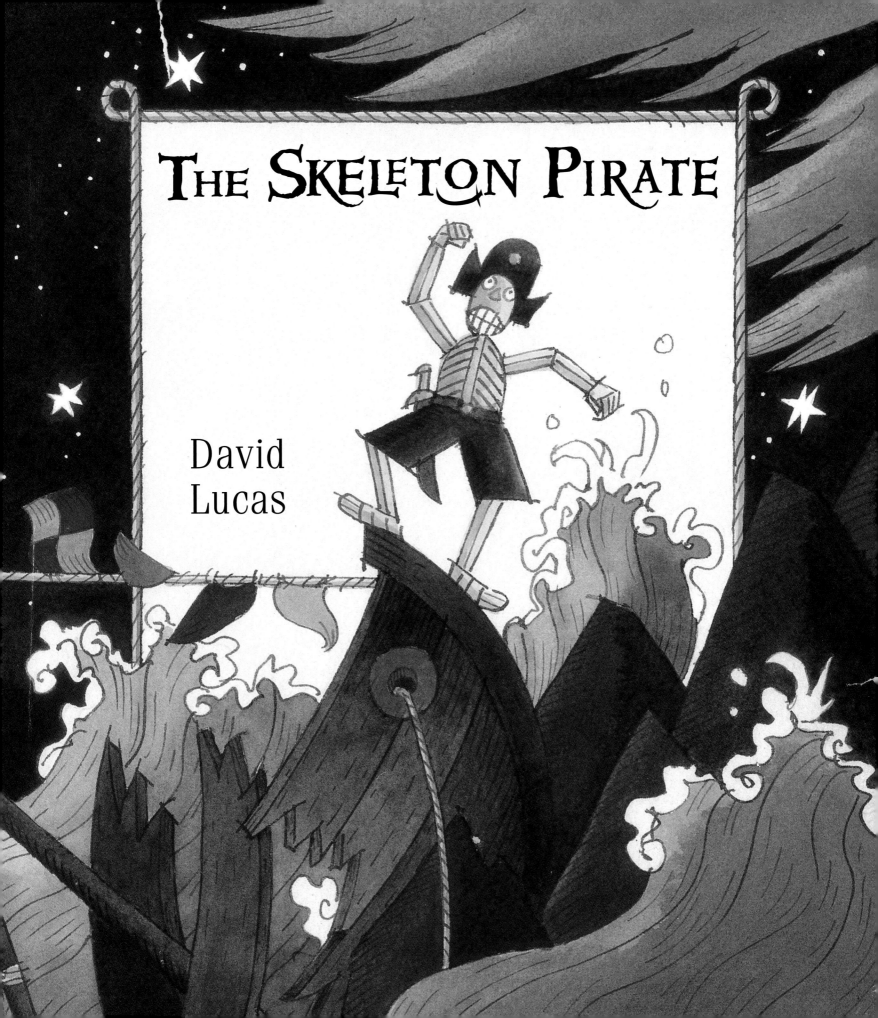

THE SKELETON PIRATE

David
Lucas

Everyone had heard of the Skeleton Pirate.
The Skeleton Pirate was the Terror of the Seas.

"I'll never be beaten!" he said.

"I'll never be beaten!"

"I'll NEVER be beaten!"

All the other pirates cheered.
"We've beaten the Skeleton Pirate
at last!"
"*Curses!*" said the Skeleton Pirate,
through gritted teeth.
"I'll never be beaten!"

"Hahaha!" they laughed
and threw him overboard.

"Hello there, my lovely!" said the Skeleton Pirate.
The Mermaid smiled. "Oh dear! It looks like
you've been beaten at last!"
"I'll never be beaten!" he said. "Would you...?
Oh, thank you, my dear..."

skeleton key

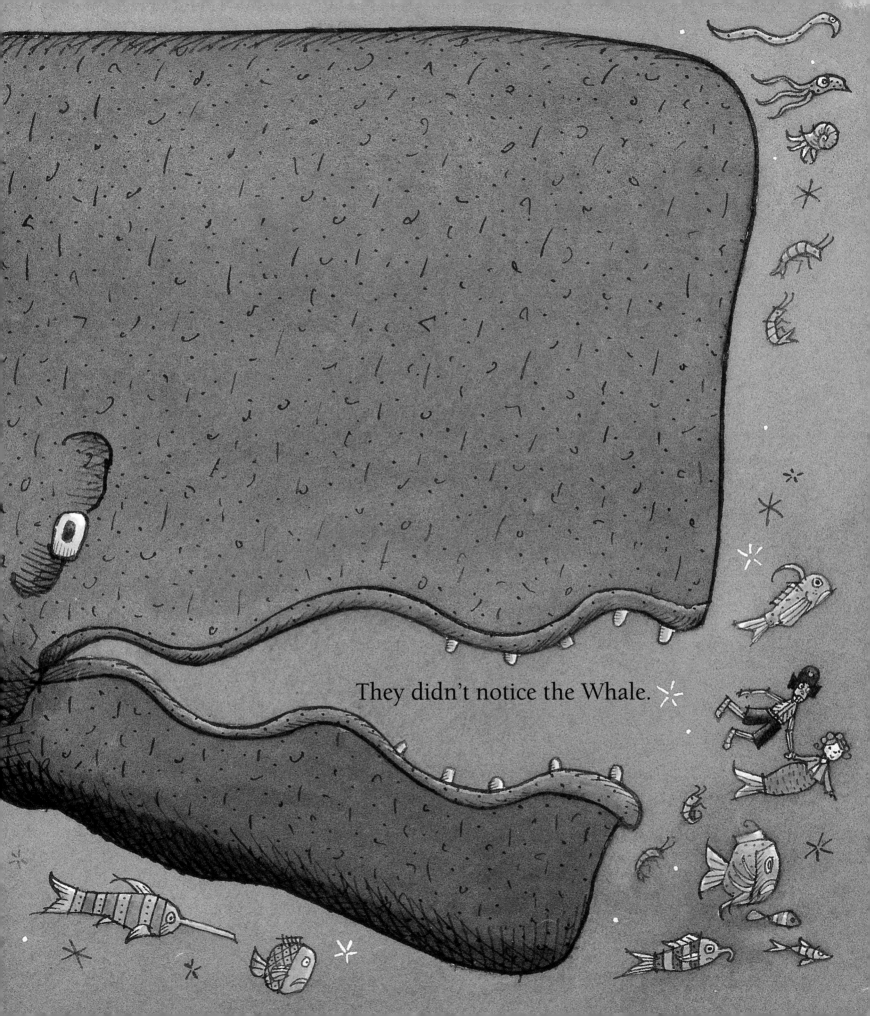

They didn't notice the Whale.

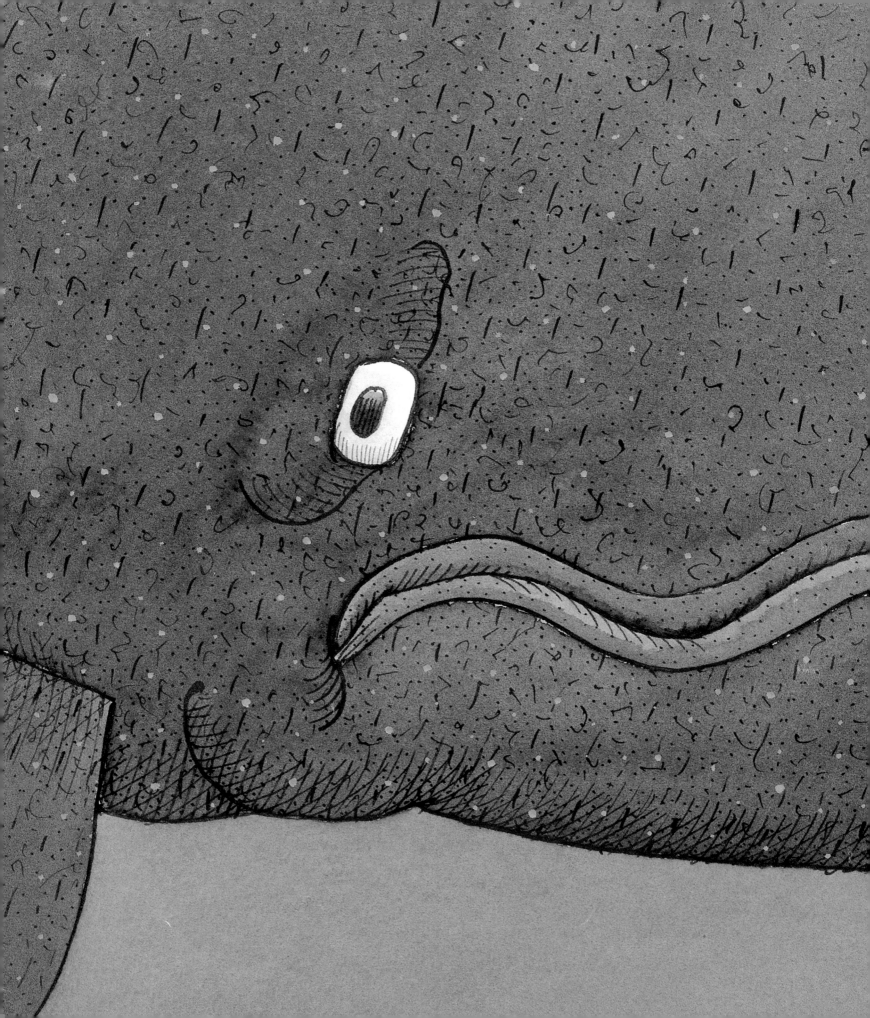

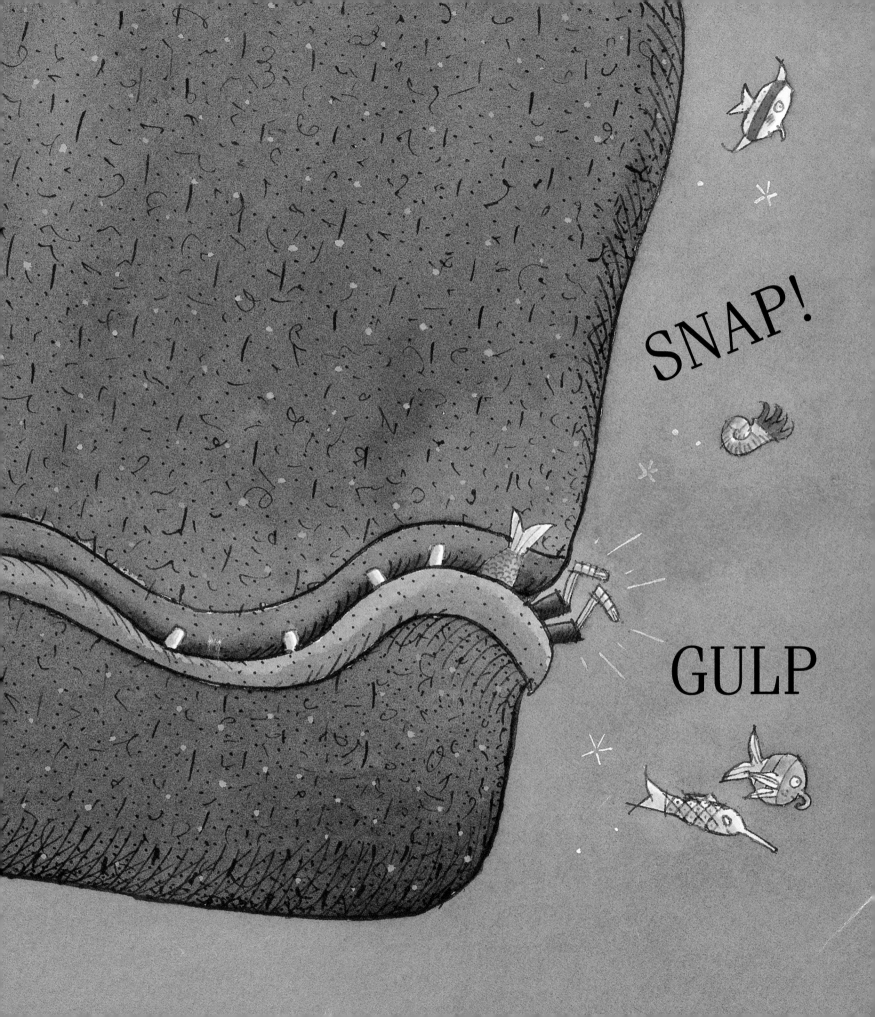

"What do we do now?" cried the Mermaid.

They were in the belly of the Whale.

"We're not beaten yet!" said the Skeleton Pirate
and he shook his fist.

"Hey, Whale! Come and fight me you big coward!"

The only sound was the Mermaid
blowing her nose.

"Perhaps fighting isn't always the answer," said the Mermaid, gently.

"What else is there?" said the Skeleton Pirate.

"*Talking?*" said the Mermaid.

"Talking!" said the Skeleton Pirate. "Of course!"

They looked at each other.

"But I don't think the Whale can hear us," said the Skeleton Pirate.

"We could speak right in his ear..." said the Mermaid.

"Where's the ear of a whale?"

"Near his brain..."

"Come on!" The Skeleton Pirate flashed his eyes.

"I've got a plan!"

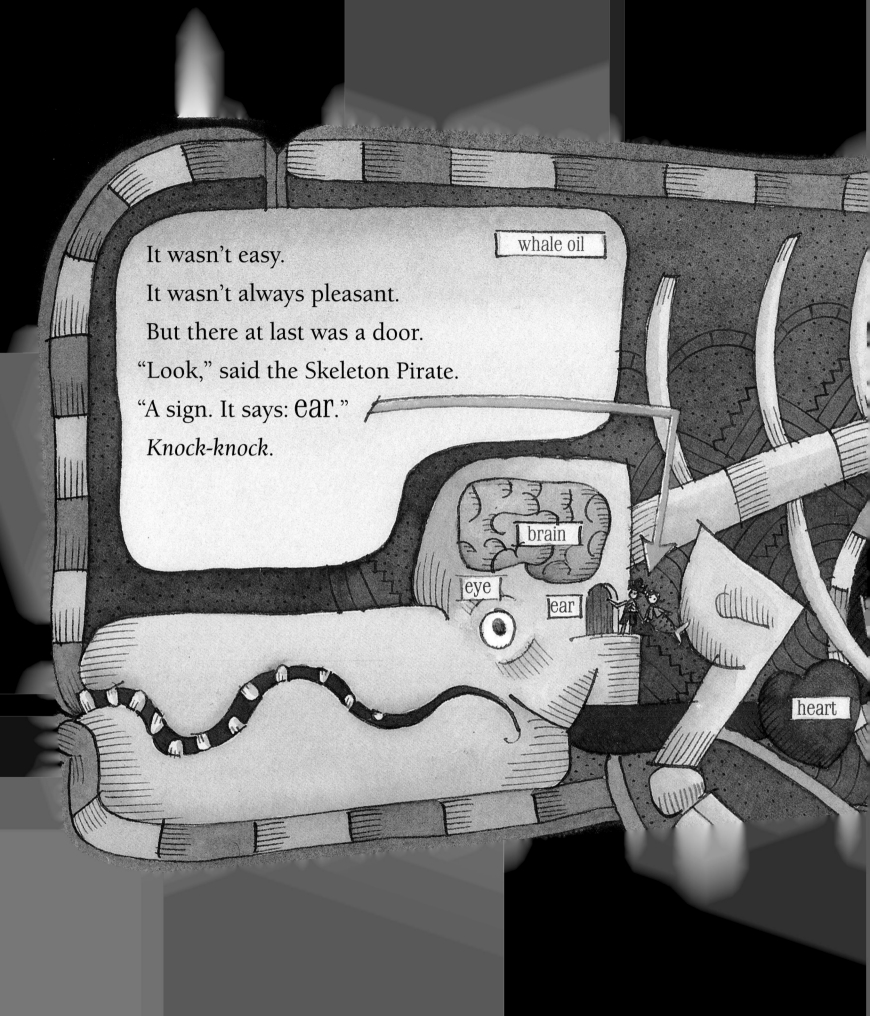

It wasn't easy.

It wasn't always pleasant.

But there at last was a door.

"Look," said the Skeleton Pirate.

"A sign. It says: ear."

Knock-knock.

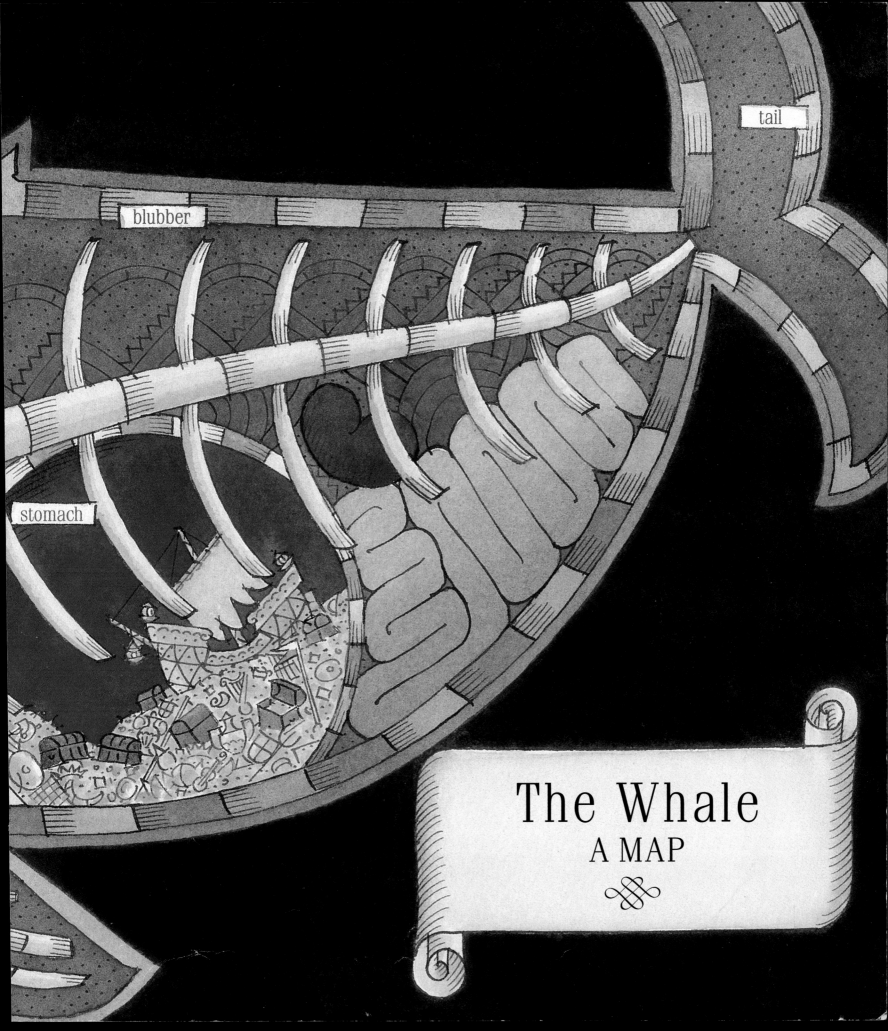

"Who's there?" boomed the Whale.

"You *ate* us," said the Skeleton Pirate.

"You swallowed us whole..."

"Oh dear, I'm terribly sorry," said the Whale. His voice echoed all around them.

"Did you know you're full of gold and treasure and jewels?" said the Skeleton Pirate.

"You even swallowed a *Golden Ship*!" said the Mermaid.

"No wonder I feel so ill," said the Whale. "I wish there was *something* somebody could do to help."

The Skeleton Pirate grinned.

"I know exactly what to do."

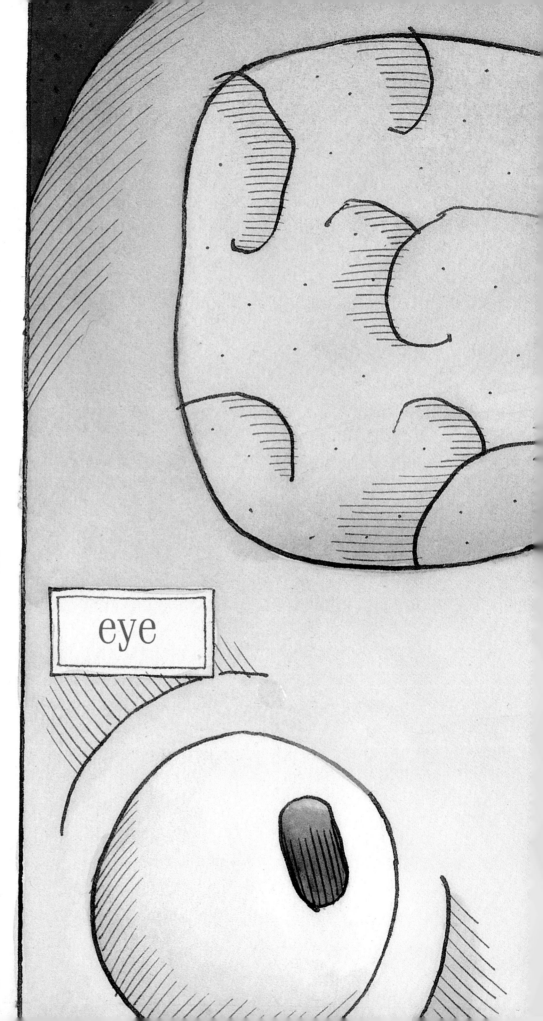

eye

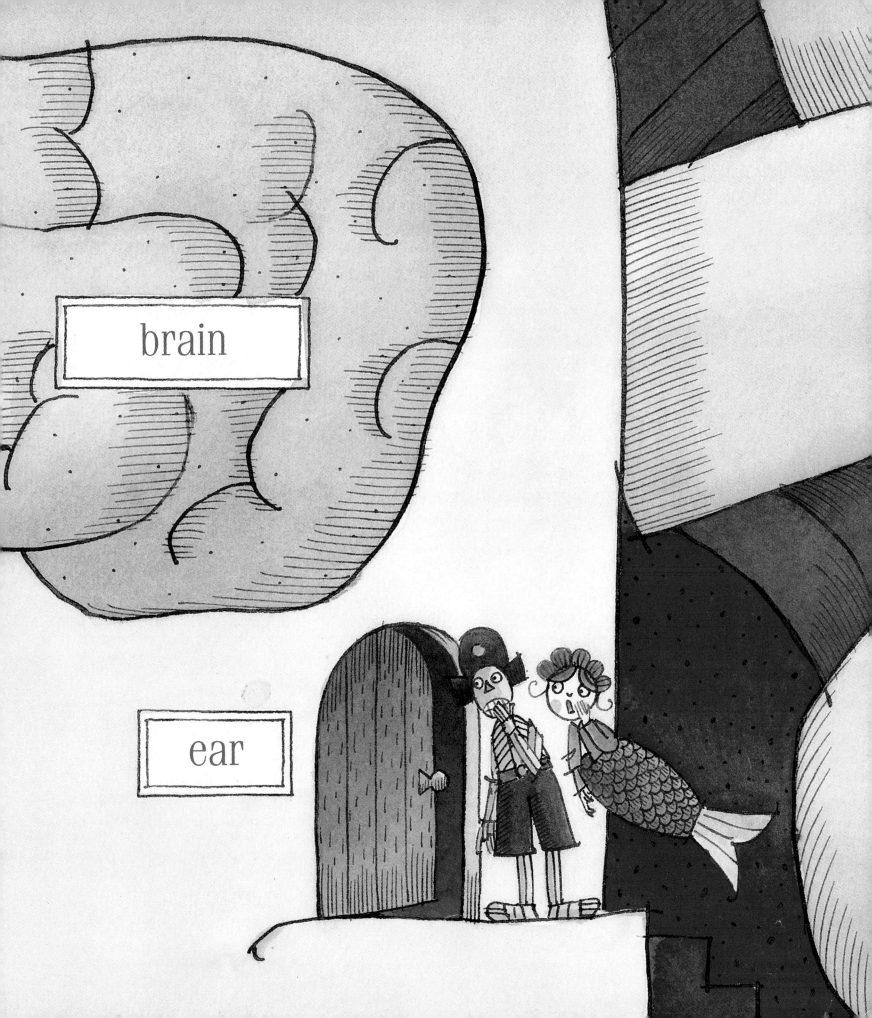

brain

ear

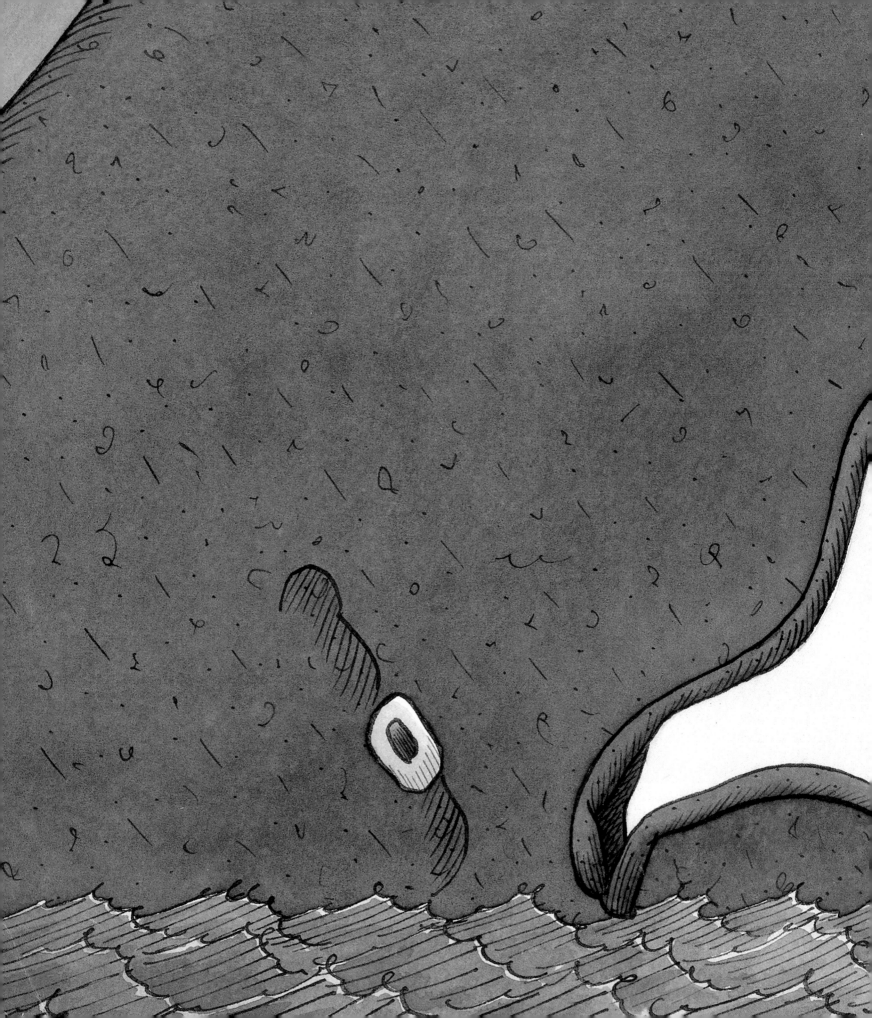

They filled the Golden Ship with treasure.
"Open wide!" cried the Skeleton Pirate.
The Whale did as he was told.

They sailed away into the sunset.

Night fell and the moon shone and the Skeleton Pirate knelt.

He looked deep into the Mermaid's eyes.

"You know," he said, "I think I've been beaten at last!"

"Don't be so silly," said the Mermaid,

and laughed...